Mr. Mustachio

Yasmin Finch & Abigail Tompkins

Mr Mustachio

is **very**, very

$$\text{tall,}$$

and **very**, very

$$\text{thin.}$$

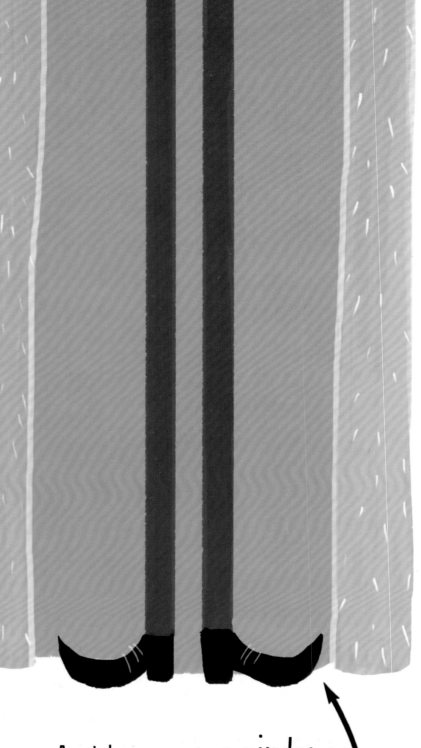

He has a coat made from camel hair, that touches the ground when he walks.

And he wears **pointy** black boots, with a small heel.

"What a perfectly fantabulous day for a picnic!" he thinks.

As Mr Mustachio marches down the street, his extra long, super-duper, curly-wurly moustache flies wildly in the wind, and he smiles with pride.

Tall children have to duck it.

Small children try to snatch at it.

Birds like to nest in it.

He packs up the picnic, runs over, and gives the
roundabout a little poke.

Mr Mustachio hops on.
"Perfect!"

He whirls round and round and round and faster and round

and faster and round and round and round and ROUND!

Oh no...

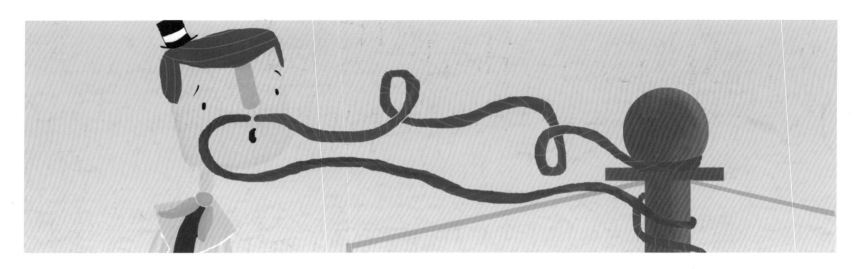

Mr Mustachio's extra long, super-duper, curly-wurly

moustache whirls round and round the roundabout's middle.

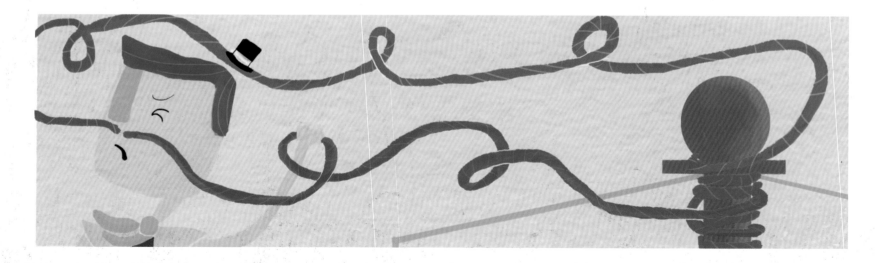

"Aghhhh!" he shouts. "Help! HELP!"
He twists. He tugs. But Mr Mustachio is
STUCK.

One super strong girl tries pulling.
Mr Mustachio stays STUCK.

Two clever boys try slippery soap.
Mr Mustachio stays stuck.

Three wise grannies try tools.
Mr Mustachio stays stuck.
"This is not fantabulous."

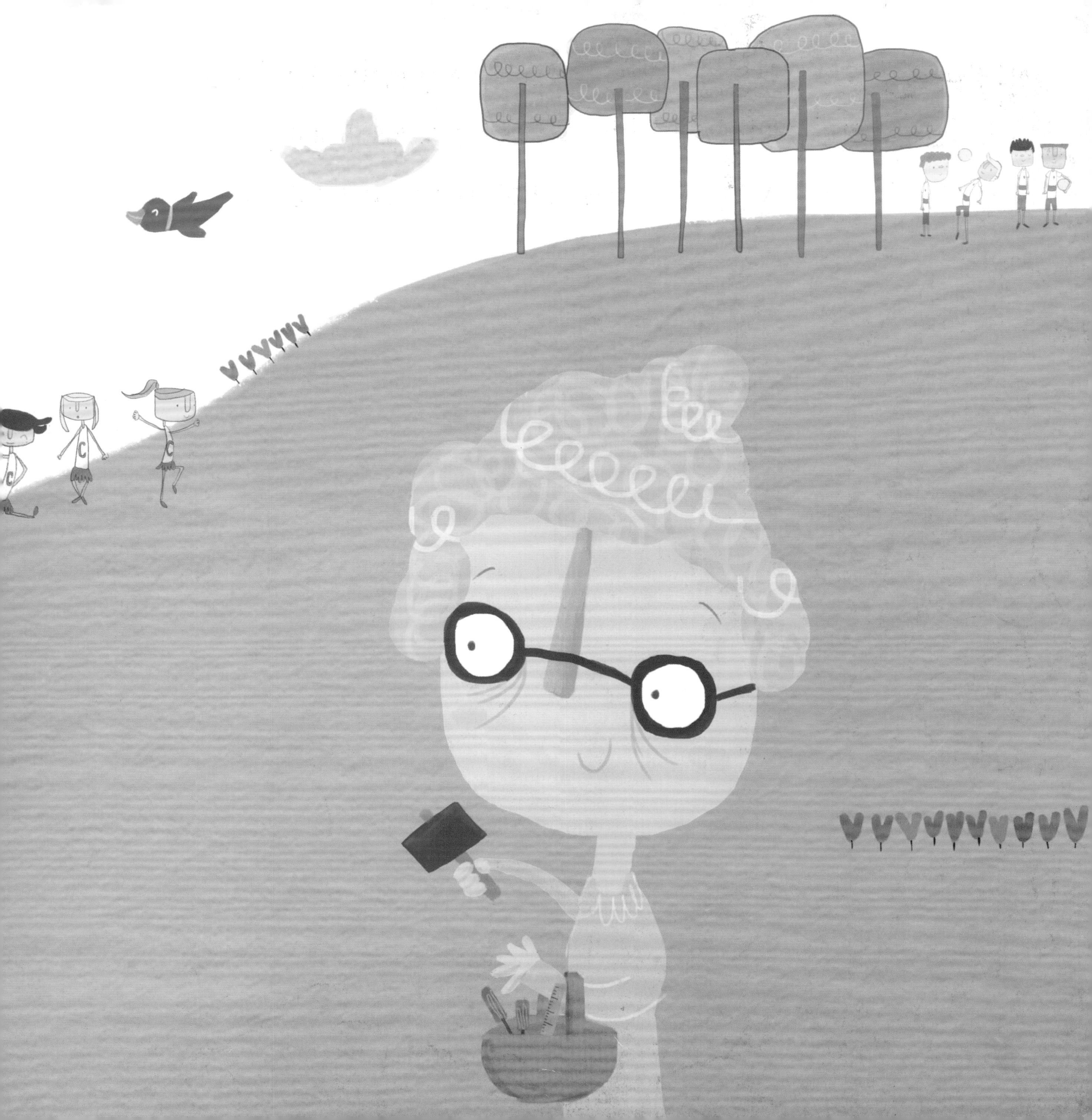

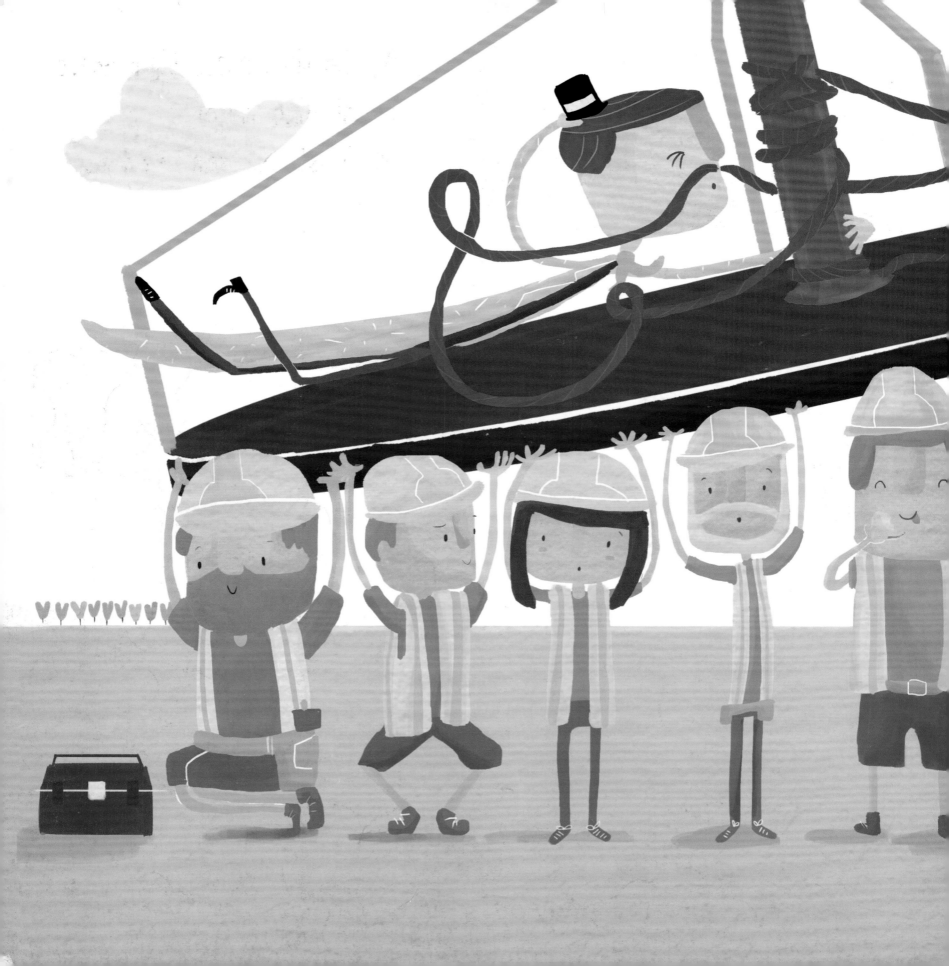

By the time nine big builders
try shaking him off,
Mr Mustachio realises that...

...one of the ten tall teachers must snip him free.

The next morning, Mr Mustachio looks in the mirror.
This will not do,

Mr Mustachio **MUST** have a moustache.
He thinks hard.

Two old toothbrushes?

NO.

Two little mice?

NO.

Two fluffy feathers?

NO.

Two stripey socks?

As Mr Mustachio marches down the street, his extra long, super-duper, stripey-wipey sock moustache flies wildly in the wind, and he smiles with pride.

"What a super simple sock solution," he says.
"Tomorrow I think I'd like
a banana one."

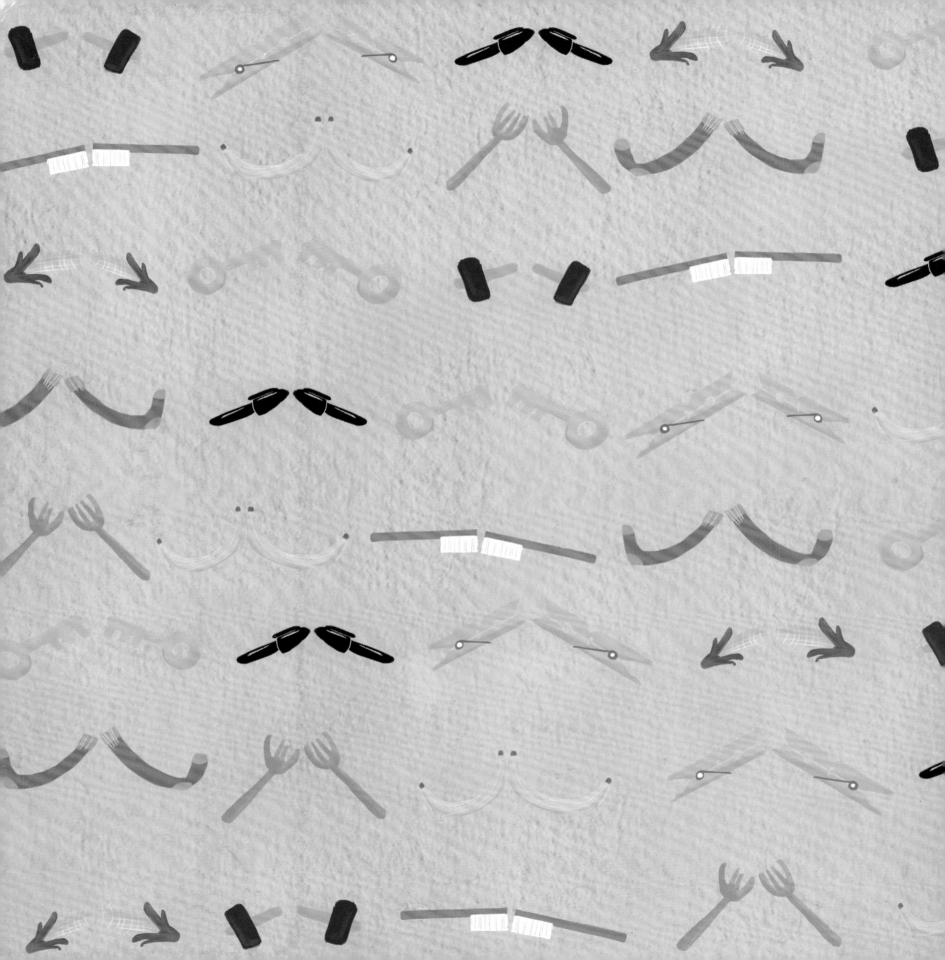

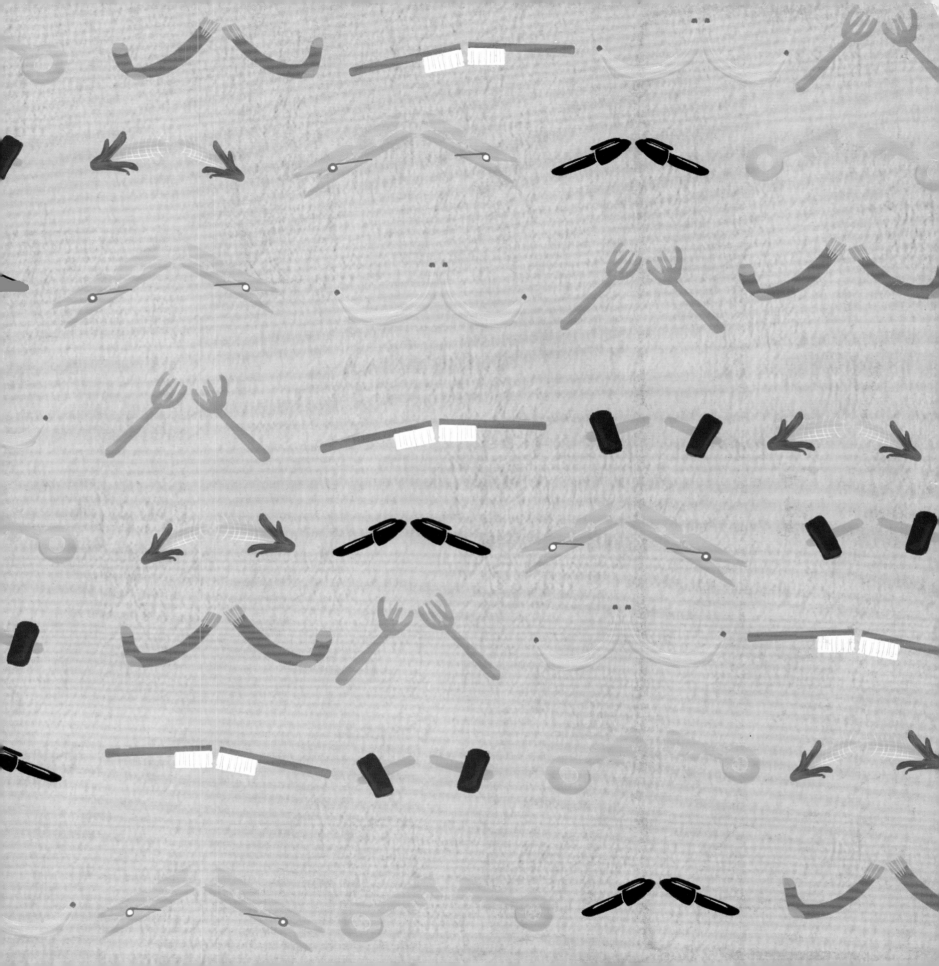

Mr Mustachio
is an original concept by
© Yasmin Finch

Illustrator: Abigail Tompkins
Represented by Plum Pudding Illustration

Published by MAVERICK ARTS PUBLISHING LTD
Studio 3A, City Business Centre, 6 Brighton Road,
Horsham, West Sussex, RH13 5BB
© Maverick Arts Publishing Limited August 2016
+44 (0)1403 256941

A CIP catalogue record for this book is available at the British Library.

ISBN 978-1-84886-220-3

Maverick
arts publishing

www.maverickbooks.co.uk